Mem Fox

A Particular Cow

Illustrated by
Terry Denton

PUFFIN BOOKS

PUFFIN BOOKS

Published by the Penguin Group
Penguin Group (Australia)
250 Camberwell Road, Camberwell, Victoria 3124, Australia
(a division of Pearson Australia Group Pty Ltd)
Penguin Group (USA) Inc.
375 Hudson Street, New York, New York 10014, USA
Penguin Group (Canada)
90 Eglinton Avenue East, Suite 700, Toronto, Canada ON M4P 2Y3
(a division of Pearson Penguin Canada Inc.)
Penguin Books Ltd
80 Strand, London WC2R 0RL England
Penguin Ireland
25 St Stephen's Green, Dublin 2, Ireland
(a division of Penguin Books Ltd)
Penguin Books India Pvt Ltd
11 Community Centre, Panchsheel Park, New Delhi - 110 017, India
Penguin Group (NZ)
67 Apollo Drive, Rosedale, North Shore 0632, New Zealand
(a division of Pearson New Zealand Ltd)
Penguin Books (South Africa) (Pty) Ltd
24 Sturdee Avenue, Rosebank, Johannesburg 2196, South Africa

Penguin Books Ltd, Registered Offices: 80 Strand, London, WC2R 0RL, England

First published in the United States by Harcourt, Inc, 2006
This edition published by Penguin Group (Australia), 2010

7 9 10 8 6

Text copyright © Mem Fox, 2006
Illustrations copyright © Terry Denton, 2006

The moral right of the author has been asserted

Design by Lauren Rille
The illustrations in this book were done in black ink and watercolour on Arches paper
Typeset in Handwriter
Printed and bound in China by Everbest Printing Co. Ltd

National Library of Australia
Cataloguing-in-Publication data:
Fox, Mem, 1946–
A particular cow/Mem Fox; illustrator, Terry Denton.

ISBN: 978 0 143 50134 3 (pbk.)
For pre-school age.
Cows – Juvenile fiction.
Denton, Terry, 1950–
A823.3

puffin.com.au

For Terry Denton,
a particular hero - M.F.

For Evie, who went
for a particular walk - T.D.

Every Saturday morning a particular cow
went for a particular walk.

Usually nothing particular happened.

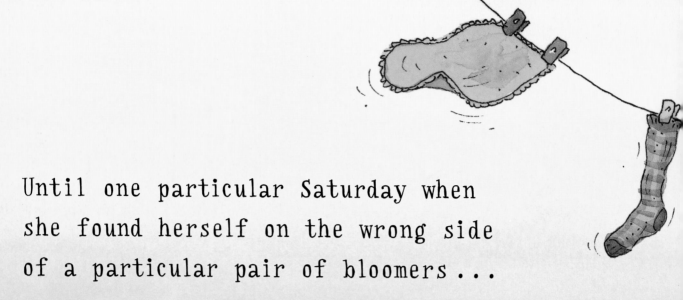

Until one particular Saturday when she found herself on the wrong side of a particular pair of bloomers...

and a particular woman...

and a particular postman...

and a particular party of children...

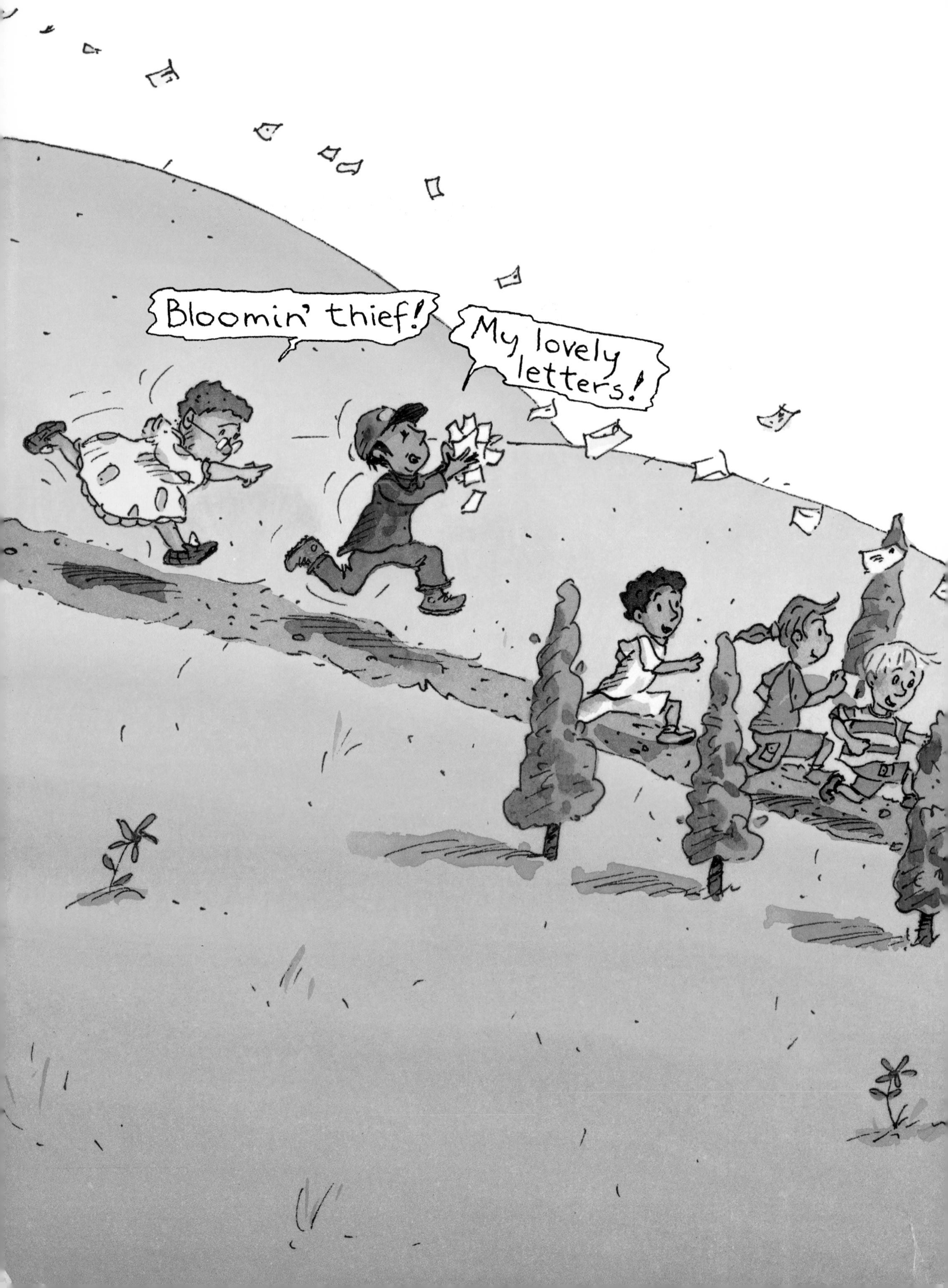
Bloomin' thief!
My lovely letters!

and a particular gang of sailors,

who almost sank in a particular river

on account of this particular cow
that we're talking about,

tossed her tail at the summer flies,

and went on her way without surprise,

on that particular Saturday morning.